P9-CFQ-297

To Paul and Dorothy—
I have always loved being your mother
—M.H.

To Holly
—R. G.

Library of Congress Cataloging-in-Publication Data Available

2 4 6 8 10 9 7 5 3

Published by Sterling Publishing Co., Inc.
387 Park Avenue South, New York, NY 10016
Text copyright © 2005 by Marie Hodge
Illustrations copyright © 2005 by Renée Graef
Distributed in Canada by Sterling Publishing
c/o Canadian Manda Group, 165 Dufferin Street
Toronto, Ontario, Canada M6K 3H6
Distributed in Great Britain and Europe by Chris Lloyd at Orca Book
Services, Stanley House, Fleets Lane, Poole BH15 3AJ, England
Distributed in Australia by Capricorn Link (Australia) Pty. Ltd.
P.O. Box 704, Windsor, NSW 2756, Australia

Printed in China
Sterling ISBN-13 978-1-4027-1265-4
ISBN-10 1-4027-1265-0

For information about custom editions, special sales, premium and
corporate purchases, please contact Sterling Special Sales
Department at 800-805-5489 or specialsales sterlingpub.com.

Are You Sleepy Yet, Petey?

By Marie Hodge
Illustrated by Renée Graef

Sterling Publishing Co., Inc.
New York

Are you sleepy yet, Petey?
Do you want to cuddle with your
blanket and go to sleep?

It's time for bed, Petey.
Close your eyes.

If you don't go to sleep
you'll be too tired to go
to the park tomorrow.

Would you like
your bear?

Little Bear wants
you to go to sleep.

And I'll give you a treat
when you wake up!

Silly Petey! You can't have
that now. Just lie back and
you'll have it soon.

Are you out of that bed?

Petey, you're making ME tired!

Okay, I'll lie down with you.
Just for a minute.

You're tired, Petey . . .
close your eyes.

Like this.

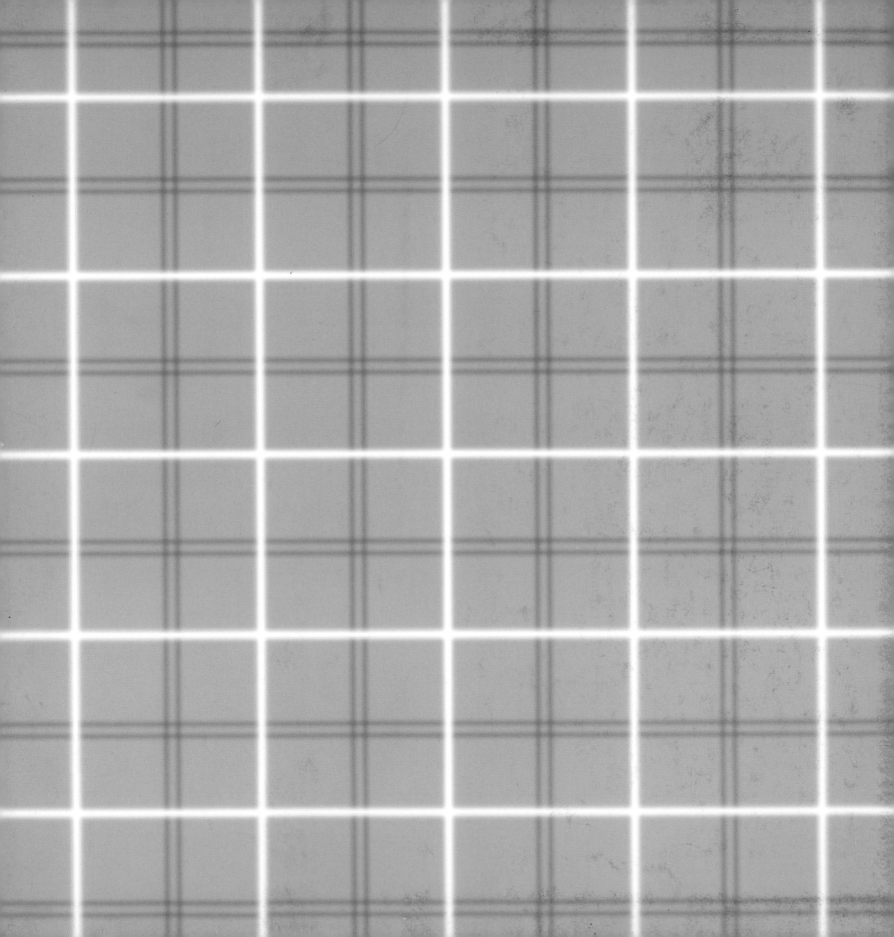